Don't miss the other stories in the
Lollapalooza short story series:

Quarantine
Common Enemies
Coiled Danger
Mars Meeting

R.W. WALLACE

AUTHOR OF THE VANGUARD

COMMON ENEMIES

A LOLLAPALOOZA SHORT STORY

BOOK 2

Common Enemies

by R.W. Wallace

Copyright © 2019 by R.W. Wallace

Copy editing by Jinxie Gervasio

Cover by the author

Cover Illustration 30745637 © 3000ad | 123rf.com

All characters and events in this book, other than those clearly in the public domain, are fictitious and any resemblance to real persons, living or dead, is purely coincidental.

All rights reserved. No part of this publication may be reproduced, distributed, or transmitted in any form or by any means, including photocopying, recording, or other electronic or mechanical methods, without the prior written permission of the publisher, except in the case of brief quotations embodied in critical reviews and certain other noncommercial uses permitted by copyright law.

www.rwwallace.com

ISBN: [979-10-95707-33-2]

Main category—Fiction

Other category—Science Fiction

First Edition

Also by R.W. Wallace

Mystery

The Tolosa Mystery Series
The Red Brick Haze (free)
The Red Brick Cellars
The Red Brick Basilica

Ghost Detective Shorts (coming soon)
Just Desserts
Lost Friends
Family Bonds
Till Death
Common Ground

Short Stories
Hidden Horrors
Cold Blue Eternity
Critters
Gertrude and the Trojan Horse
First Impressions
Let Them Eat Cake
Two's Company

Science Fiction (short stories)
The Vanguard

Adventure (short stories)
Size Matters

Fantasy (short stories)
Morbier Impossible
A Second Chance
Unexpected Consequences

COMMON ENEMIES

The piston shot out of the long, black tube, slowed just before reaching its zenith, then sped back down into its holster. It repeated the action once, twice...

"That's how a piston is supposed to work," Yosu Gaal said to his audience of two. He followed the movement with his eyes for a few moments longer, happy to be working with machines again.

Machines were predictable. Logical. With the right tools, machines could be fixed. An hour ago, this piston made a scratching sound every time it shot out; now it flowed smoothly from one position to the next, with only an accompanying, soft *swish*.

The piston was one of twenty, part of the large machine responsible for cleaning and circulating the air throughout the space ship, and absolutely essential for their survival. They covered both sides of the hallway-like room, each piston starting its downward movement when the one before it was halfway down.

The resulting ballet was more beautiful than anything Yosu had seen in any theater around the universe.

Except the sea-creatures on Galatassy. Their sense of timing and precision was uncanny.

Yosu turned to face his students. He couldn't remember their names to save his life, and had taken to calling them Shorty and Shorter, which probably wouldn't do in the long run. They'd come aboard the Lollapalooza from a planet named Fortlite372 two days ago, and Yosu suspected they'd been selected because they were the shortest creatures available.

On Fortlite372, your height was equivalent to your worth, and Yosu and his captain hadn't exactly made any friends while they were there.

"Every system aboard a ship like the Lollapalooza is doubled," Yosu explained. "This, so the backup can take over if the primary ever breaks down." He put a loving hand on the closest hydraulic pump. "This system is quadrupled. Air is not to be trifled with."

Shorty and Shorter nodded, their tiny eyes darting from one piston to another.

They were bright enough creatures, and willing to work once they understood a task. The problem was making sure that they had, indeed, understood what he asked of them. Clearly, where they came from, asking questions was a sign of weakness, and to be avoided at all costs. Admitting ignorance seemed to be only slightly better.

It didn't make Yosu's task of training them any easier, but they *were* helping. He'd strung together his first five consecutive hours of sleep in almost a week just a few hours ago, and he felt ready to take on just about anything.

"Yosu," his captain's voice sounded in his ear piece. "We'll arrive on Harry652 tomorrow. We need to recruit and train twenty-six people. I'm putting you in charge."

Except that. Yosu couldn't do that.

ଓ

"You can't put me in charge of the crew," Yosu said to Captain Kovak—Arleen—as he slid into the copilot's chair.

The captain sat bent over one of her screens, scrolling through what seemed to be a shopping list. Her light brown hair was in its usual ponytail, which usually started out firm in the morning, but was more a general gathering of her hair down the middle of her back at this time of night. Yosu had considered the possibility of buying her a more solid hair tie, something that would hold for more than an hour, but he didn't know how to approach the subject without offending her.

"Who else am I supposed to put in charge?" the captain asked, her eyes still on her screen. "Hunkigolo Vladimolo?"

Yosu grimaced. "Which one of them is that? Shorty, or Shorter?"

Arleen raised her exasperated gaze to meet Yosu's. "That's what you're calling them?"

Yosu shrugged. "I was never any good with names. Or people." He made sure she saw his earnestness. "Which is why you can't leave me in charge of the crew."

The captain threw her hands in the air. "Well, I'm not going to do it. I'm already in over my head trying to get this ship to go where I want it to and not crash into anything. I can't train a crew at the same time."

Yosu eyed the dashboard and its numerous screens flashing with information. Why couldn't his job be to work with logical and soulless computers?

"Oh, no, you don't," the captain said, narrowing her eyes at him. "Navigating is the captain's job. So unless you're planning to mutiny…"

Yosu raised his hands in surrender. "The Lollapalooza is all yours, Captain." Chills ran down his spine at the idea of being responsible for an entire ship and crew again.

The captain rolled her eyes at him, clearly thinking the chills were faked.

Yosu didn't correct her.

"Seriously, though, Captain," Yosu said. "I shouldn't be in charge of the crew."

She was back to studying her shopping list but glanced at Yosu at this. "Why ever not?"

Yosu ground his teeth together, wishing he had gum. He'd planned to replenish his stock on Fortlite372, but between being put in quarantine and arm-wrestling for the right to leave, there just hadn't been an opportunity. Now he found himself chewing thin air whenever his mind wandered too far.

"I'm no good with people," he replied. "Not exactly born to be a leader."

"Not good with people," the captain repeated, as if trying to make sense of them by saying them out loud. "You were the most popular guy on the ship when there were thirty of us. You have all that"—she waved her hand to encompass all of

Yosu—"mysterious thing going. All the guys wanted to be you, and all the girls wanted in your pants. A couple of the guys, too, actually, if I'm not mistaken."

Yosu's stare was flat. "Are you telling me they liked me because they *didn't* know me?"

The captain scrunched up her nose and tipped her head from side to side as she thought about it. "Maybe? I mean, you don't need to tell everyone your deepest, darkest secrets in order to be a good leader. In fact, the opposite is probably true."

Sighing, with both elbows on his knees, Yosu folded his hands and bowed his head so he wouldn't have to meet his captain's eyes. "That's not why I don't want to be in charge of the new crew."

"Then why?"

The silence stretched, as Yosu thought of and rejected possible explanations. The only sound was of the air conditioning overhead, and the ship's engines rumbling at the back of the ship. Yosu started chewing on nothing several times and wondered if his captain would think him crazy for it.

"Unless you can come up with a valid reason for why I shouldn't put you in charge," the captain said, "you'll be going to that recruitment booth on Harry652 and bring us back a full crew." She tentatively put her hand on top of Yosu's folded ones. "It can be scary to be in charge of the training and well-being of so many people. But I believe in you. I have no doubt you can do it."

Yosu thought back to his three years as captain. Sure, he was a good captain. He'd even go so far as to say his crew loved him.

Right up until the moment he got everyone killed.

☙

The recruitment "booth" wasn't aptly named.

At the outskirts of the planet's capital, it consisted of three enormous warehouses. One was for humans and sufficiently similar, one for what most people still just called aliens because they were so different—but quite often equally useful—and one for animals. That last one was always a little in flux, since not everyone agreed on the difference between alien and animal. It was usually up to the local authorities to decide, and from what Yosu saw of the creatures present in the "animal" warehouse on Harry652, this wasn't a place he wanted to linger.

Yosu wouldn't mind going to the alien warehouse before leaving, to see if they had any interesting creatures—like that dog-like alien he'd worked with on his very first mission, who fed off dust motes. He'd never seen a cleaner ship.

But first: he needed twenty-six human (or similar) crew members. Some captains liked working with a mostly alien crew, but Captain Kovak was sufficiently new at this not to want to add any risk factors that weren't necessary.

In fact, she'd prepared Yosu with a shopping list of potential new hires. She'd ordered them by preference, and added little comments here and there, then given Yosu "free rein" to hire whoever he thought would best fit.

Yosu would have found it funny, except he felt infinitely grateful to his captain for doing the choosing for him.

Popping a brand new chewing-gum in his mouth—peppermint flavored to feel fresh for a day of negotiating—Yosu pushed open the door to the "human" warehouse.

A wall of noise slammed into him the second he opened the door. There must be over two hundred people in the one giant space, and they were all talking, some in a normal voice, some shouting so hard Yosu's throat constricted in sympathy.

A hallway of sorts ran down the center of the warehouse. On each side, tables stood back to back, creating the world's longest counters. Behind each table sat a negotiator, easily identifiable by their trademark red berets, screens spread across their tables, showing head shots, background information, weapons training, engineering degrees… anything a hiring captain could want to know.

Behind the line of negotiators, couches, chairs, tables, stools—anything adapted for waiting, really—were spread across the space with no particular order. This was where the potential hires hung out, while waiting to be called in by a negotiator.

A good two thirds of the seats were occupied. Yosu figured he'd have a good chance of picking up all of the captain's top picks.

Then he'd figure out to which of them he could hand off his responsibilities to.

☙

Anouk Roux had pink shoulder-length hair, purple eyebrows, and a yellow fluorescent tracksuit. Her eyes, which would normally have drawn attention because they were such a light gray they almost faded into the whites, disappeared in the mass of colors. Her biceps showed through the jacket of the tracksuit, and her thighs bulged every time she shifted on her chair.

If Yosu were to go up against *this* woman in a race or in a match of arm-wrestling, he would lose, no doubt about it.

"So you're a mechanic?" Yosu asked, dropping his gaze to the tablet in front of him in order to avoid staring rudely.

"Yup," Anouk replied. "Grew up in the bowels of my dad's spaceship. Learned from the best mechanics around. Repaired my first fuel pump when I was five. Built an engine running on solar power when I was ten." She leaned back so she was balancing on the two back feet of her chair.

Yosu glanced at the information the negotiator had prepared for him. Anouk was apparently twenty-seven. He'd have believed anything between eighteen and forty. The dyed hair and eyebrows really threw him off.

She'd worked on ten different spaceships over the last decade, and though she had impressive references from all of her former captains, this raised a red flag for Yosu.

"I see you've never stayed with a captain for more than fourteen months," he said. "Is there a particular reason for that?"

Anouk's lips lifted in half a smirk. "I didn't get kicked off the ship, if that's what you're worried about." She rolled her shoulders and tipped her head back to look up at the warehouse's ceiling a hundred feet above them. "I guess I get bored," she finally said. "When there's nothing new to learn from the other mechanics working on the ship—or the actual mechanics of the ship—my mind wanders, and not long after my body follows suit."

Yosu frowned. "Then why should I hire you for the Lollapalooza?"

Her smile had a hefty dose of arrogance, but it seemed genuine nonetheless. "Because I'm worth the investment." She let her chair down to the ground and leaned across the table to look Yosu in the eyes. "I don't just look at what other mechanics have done and learn from that. I improve on what I see. And I share with my colleagues. So even if I stay with you for only six months, it'll be worth it because your engine will need less fuel, your hydraulics will break down less frequently, and your capacity of flying under the radar in most of the universe will greatly improve."

"Really?" Yosu's eyebrows shot up. "You know stealth?"

Anouk's smile widened, showing what appeared to be a pink diamond on one of her upper molars. "I know *everything*, honey."

Yosu chewed on his gum for a few moments while he considered. Even if some of it *was* just arrogance talking, it seemed like she'd be worth the investment.

"You never call me honey again, and we have a deal," he said, offering his hand for her to shake.

"Deal." She shook his hand. Though the look she gave him made Yosu doubt it was the last time he'd hear that particular endearment.

Yosu rose to move on to the next negotiator, but before leaving, he asked, "Who's your dad, by the way? He must have had one hell of a ship."

Anouk's smile dropped and she seemed to really see Yosu for the first time. "He did," she said. "And he was one hell of a captain. His name was Captain Marc Roux. But everyone just called him Barberousse."

Yosu nodded and moved away from the table. He pretended to know where he was going, when in reality he couldn't even remember why he was here. He felt lightheaded and wasn't sure he could feel his legs.

Barberousse.

The only man who might carry as much of the blame of that fateful day as Yosu.

And one of that day's casualties.

ଔ

FOR THE FIRST time since their old crew had been wiped out by a particularly nasty version of the flu two weeks ago, the mess was full of laughing and eating crew members, knives and forks clattering against plates, glasses clinking in toasts, and a chef yelling at people to shut up and enjoy their food.

Although Yosu was thrilled to eat foot prepared by a professional and relieved to be able to fit in eight-hour nights of sleep, he couldn't get rid of the growing ball of fear and guilt in his stomach. It grew bigger for every time he saw Anouk's pink hair and was putting a serious dent in Yosu's appetite.

"You're not eating much," Captain Kovak said. She sat next to Yosu, at the head of the table, and had just wolfed down an impressively large steak, two oven-baked potatoes, and a mountain of green salad. Now she leaned back in her chair, smoothing a hand across her belly.

Yosu shrugged. "Not really hungry today," he said.

"You didn't eat much yesterday, either." The captain might look like she was lazing around after a full meal, but her blue eyes missed nothing as they studied Yosu.

"Maybe I caught a stomach bug on Harry652, or something." Yosu pushed at his potato with his fork, moving it to the other side of the plate.

"Odd that nobody else caught it, then."

"Mhm."

The chatter around them continued as Yosu moved food around on his plate, and the captain sipped water from her glass.

"Did you empty out Harry652's stock of chewing gum?" Captain Kovak asked, a glint in her eye.

"What?" Yosu looked up at her in confusion. "No. They had plenty."

"So you're not out of the stuff, then? I haven't seen you chew one in two days."

Yosu swallowed. The captain was too observant. Yosu had enough chewing gum to last him for close to a year. But he'd realized that he chewed like his life depended on it whenever Anouk was in his line of sight, and it was too much of a giveaway. Instead, he found himself chewing on his bottom lip—which might not be much of an improvement.

"Just taking a break," he mumbled.

"Uh huh." The captain snapped her back straight as she caught sight of something behind Yosu's back. "Ensign Roux," she called. "Have a seat over here, will you?"

"Sure thing, Captain." Anouk came into view, her yellow tracksuit the first thing Yosu's eyes snatched on, her pink hair a quick second.

Yosu started chewing on his lip, realized the captain noticed, and promptly forced his mouth to stop moving.

Anouk set her plate down across from Yosu and flopped into her chair. "What's up, Captain. Anything in need of fixing?"

The captain smiled. "I'm sure there are lots of things in need of repair, but that's not why I called you over. I trust my team of mechanics to take care of my ship."

Anouk didn't say anything, but she seemed happy with the captain's answer. She dug into her steak with an enthusiasm to rival the captain's.

"Rumor has it," the captain said, "you're the daughter of the infamous Barberousse?"

Anouk kept her focus on her food. "Rumor has it right. Though I'm not sure it really qualifies as a rumor since I'm the one who told Gaal here about it." She used her knife to point at Yosu.

"Did you now." The captain met Yosu's gaze, a slight lift of her eyebrow asking him why he hadn't told her.

Yosu shrugged, as if to say he hadn't deemed it important.

"Barberousse was a world-renowned pirate," the captain said.

"Sure was," Anouk agreed.

"But you appear to have always kept on the right side of the law."

Lifting a shoulder in a shrug, Anouk finished chewing before answering. "Except for when I worked on my dad's ship, yeah. But I wouldn't read too much into it. I just realized not fearing for my life allowed me to spend more time with the machines." She took a sip of water. "And having your machinery blown to bits every few weeks is bloody annoying."

The captain chuckled. "I can imagine."

Pausing for a moment, Anouk looked the captain in the eye. "You don't need to worry about me turning rouge, or leading a mutiny, Captain. I'm here to work. When I get tired of your ship, I'll leave, but not without notice."

The captain nodded in satisfaction. "I appreciate your honesty, Ensign Roux. Now." She slapped her hands on the table and pushed herself up. "I'm going back to the cockpit. Gaal, keep our new mechanic company, will you? Maybe her appetite will inspire you to finish your own plate."

Clenching his teeth together, Yosu nodded. He recognized an order when he heard one.

But his appetite was long gone.

☙

"So, what does the captain want us to talk about?" Anouk kept her focus on her food, but she glanced up at Yosu as she asked the question.

"What?" Yosu chewed on his lip, noticed he did it, and stopped. Then started chewing again.

This was pointless. Giving up on his resolution, Yosu searched his pockets until he found a packet of gum and popped one into his mouth.

Anouk set her knife and fork on her plate and crossed her arms, elbows on the table. "The captain could have asked me about my dad anytime. She made me eat here because she wants us to talk."

Could the captain really be that observant?

Not observant enough to know that what Yosu really needed was to be as far away from Barberousse's daughter as possible.

"I don't know what's going on in the captain's head," he said, avoiding meeting Anouk's eyes.

"Maybe not, but something's definitely going on in yours, though." Anouk pulled her hair behind her ears, making the pink strands sway above her shoulders. "Whenever I'm in a room, you find an excuse to leave. If I'm eating when you arrive in here, you take your meal to your room." She looked at Yosu's mostly empty plate. "Or maybe you don't eat at all. What on Earth did I do to affect you this strongly?"

Yosu had to give her an answer she'd find believable. After only a week together on board the Lollapalooza, he'd learned to know her well enough to realize she wouldn't let go until she'd cracked the mystery. Mostly, she applied this stubbornness to solving mechanical issues, but she'd also gotten a particularly depressed crew member to open up about his recent divorce, making him, if not exactly joyous, at least less of a drag.

"The color of your—"

"I know I'm visually loud," she cut him off. "But that's not the issue here."

Yosu chewed his gum until he feared for his teeth's wellbeing and didn't even try to stop.

She couldn't learn the truth. "You're a very beautiful—"

"I know I'm gorgeous, honey." She winked, but her expression stayed serious. "But you're attracted to the captain, not me. Next."

"I'm not... How did you..." Yosu's breath came out in an explosive *whoosh*. "You're impossible," he mumbled, his face on fire and his thumping heart almost overruling the guilt in his stomach.

Almost.

"Maybe I don't want to tell you," Yosu said. "I'm your superior officer. I could just order you never to talk to me again."

Anouk rolled her clear, gray eyes. "That'd be the stupidest order you've ever given. And you know it."

"God, you're frustrating," Yosu said, putting his head in his hands. "You're worse than your father," he whispered.

The minute the words were out of his mouth, he clamped his lips shut and wished he could take them back. Perhaps she hadn't heard?

"You knew my father?"

No such luck.

ೞ

Yosu assumed the rest of the crew continued talking and eating around them, but he couldn't tell because his ears were ringing. He couldn't see anything beyond Anouk, and even she was a blurry mix of fluorescent yellow and pink.

"How did you know my father?" Anouk asked again. Her voice was calm; she didn't seem angry—yet.

Yosu chewed his gum and shook his head.

They sat like that for several minutes, Anouk calmly looking at Yosu, and Yosu frenetically chewing his gum.

"*When* did you know my father?"

Yosu met her clear eyes, even managed to focus on them, but no words came out of his mouth. His pulse was off the charts.

"You were there the day he died, weren't you?"

Yosu gulped.

Anouk nodded. "Were you on his crew?"

Yosu shook his head.

"Well, that's a relief," Anouk said lightly. "Or I'd have had to kill you."

She studied Yosu, taking in the sweat on his forehead, his panicked eyes, his manic chewing. "You think I'm going to kill you anyway."

More chewing. He needed a new gum—this one was turning into stone—but didn't think he had the necessary coordination to get one out of his pocket, out of the packet, and into his mouth.

"So you were with the opposing crew? The police?"

Yosu didn't trust his voice, so he kept his replies to shaking or nodding his head—and right now he nodded—but he was starting to accept that this conversation was really happening.

He hadn't just been *with* the other crew, of course. He'd been their commanding officer.

Anouk sat silent, studying Yosu, as the mass emptied. When they were the only ones left, she turned to yell to the chef, "Gerard, would you mind closing the door for a minute, darling?"

"Sure thing!" Gerard called back, and the kitchen door slammed shut.

Only the whirring of the air conditioner remained.

"Someday I'm going to figure out how to get that thing to make less noise," Anouk said. "It's just air—I don't see why it has to make noise."

Yosu stayed silent.

"So you were with the police," Anouk said. She sat back in her chair, hands folded in her yellow lap. "And I'm guessing you're feeling guilty about being a participant in the battle that killed my dad? Or you're just scared that little me is going to exact my revenge on you?

"You do realize, Gaal, that I'm well aware of the type of person my father was. He was a pirate, and a damned good one—which meant that he had a shit-ton of enemies, and the police running after him twenty-four seven.

"He knew the risks, and so did I. I might have grown up on his ship, and loved his crew like they were family, but the moment I had enough experience to go work on a law-abiding vessel, I took it."

Yosu found his voice. "That's not how you explained it to the captain."

A smile pulled at the corners of her mouth. "You're not the only one who likes to keep some mystery about them, honey."

Anouk spread her hands. "So you were there the day the police finally caught up with my dad. So what? You should be happy to still be alive. From what I heard, only a handful of people survived. Two from my dad's ship and three from the police vessel. One of them, the captain, apparently."

Yosu decided he didn't care if he ridiculed himself and pulled out a new gum. His hands might have shook a little, and he got two instead of his usual one, but he got the job done. Fresh mint in his mouth, he breathed a little easier.

"The only guy," Anouk continued, "who should feel any responsibility for the loss of life that day—in addition to my dad, that goes without saying—is the captain of that police vessel. If he hadn't been so trigger happy, my dad and his crew might have been in jail instead of in a cemetery."

Yosu choked on his gum. It lodged in his throat, not letting the least bit of air through.

Yosu thumped his own chest.

Tried swallowing.

Hand to his throat, he looked to Anouk, whose eyes were wide and mouth slightly open.

"Are you choking?" she asked.

Yosu nodded and started clawing on his throat.

"Shit." Anouk jumped to her feet, rounded the table, and gave Yosu's back a good thump.

The gum dislodged from Yosu's throat and flew halfway across the room, to land with a splat on the kitchen door.

Anouk and Yosu stared at it for a moment, while Yosu caught his breath.

"Thanks," he whispered as Anouk returned to her seat.

"Any time," Anouk replied. "So you were the captain, huh?"

Yosu briefly thought of denying it—his name never appeared on any reports, as was the protocol in the interstellar police—but he was tired of worrying about what would happen if Anouk found out. What was the worst that could happen?

Guess he was about to find out.

He didn't answer but let her read it on his face when he met her eyes across the table.

Her voice was low and even, totally calm. "You must've been a damned young captain."

"Youngest captain in the police force since it was created two hundred years ago," Yosu replied. There was no pride in his words, no showing off. Just fact.

Yosu thought she'd ask about what happened that day, what led up to it, what gave his dad away.

She went straight for the heart. "Why'd you shoot?"

And that *was* the crux of it, wasn't it?

Who cared how he knew where the pirates would be? Who cared why he decided to go after them? Who cared who the snitch was on the pirate's ship?

The only thing that mattered was that the police had fired first, at the worst possible time, and the result had been a carnage.

Yosu lowered his head into his hands. "If you only knew how many times I've gone over everything we did that day, over and over, wondering how I could have prevented that first shot from going off. The answer, unfortunately, isn't all that simple."

"Did you pull the trigger?"

Yosu shook his head. "The captain runs the ship, not the guns. But it was still my fault."

Anouk considered his words for a few moments. "How is it your fault?"

"It's always the captain's fault. He's responsible for everyone and everything on his vessel."

"Fair enough." Anouk sighed. "But you can hardly be blamed if one of your crew members suddenly thinks it's a great idea to shoot at a spaceship equipped to fight off entire fleets."

"I can if I was the one to hire and train him."

Now that she knew this much, Yosu might as well tell her everything. "I realized he wasn't quite...stable...a couple of weeks after hiring him. But it was his first job, and he was so happy to finally be a real police officer, I didn't have the heart to send him back home. I figured he'd learn the ropes soon enough. That he wouldn't be so nervous whenever there was the slightest sign of danger.

"We caught up with Barberousse before he could reach that point. And since I hadn't informed my gunner that this particular ensign shouldn't be allowed close to the guns in any stressful situation, when I told the team to be ready, they gave guns to *everyone*."

He raised his head to look into Anouk's eyes. "That whole disaster could have been avoided if I'd listened to my gut and gotten rid of the ensign as soon as I realized he was unstable, or if I'd at least communicated all the vital information I had to my team. I did neither, and now they're all dead."

"Not all," Anouk said. "There were five survivors."

She didn't appear upset about Yosu's confession. Growing up on a pirate ship probably taught you to keep your cards close to your chest.

Yosu gave a mirthless laugh. "A worthless captain who quit as soon as he found someone to hand his resignation to. The stressed-out shit who pulled the trigger and caused the whole thing. Our cook—which was actually a God-send, because she is the mother of four and it would have killed me to have to tell her family she'd been killed. And the two snitches from the pirate ship."

Anouk's eyebrows shot together. "Snitches?"

"Yes. The two contacts who helped us catch up to Barberousse. They negotiated clean records in return for information on their captain's next destinations." When Anouk remained still as a statue, he asked, "You didn't know that? It's part of the public record."

"No, it's not," she whispered. "No mention of snitches."

Yosu's breath caught. "Really? But I thought…"

Yosu had only read the detailed reports and the top-secret record, since he was the one giving all the details that were in there. He hadn't read the public one but had always assumed that the reason they'd known where to show up in the first place would be part of the record.

"Who was it?" Anouk's voice went down an octave, in stark contrast to her bright clothing and hair.

"Uh…" If it wasn't part of the public record, he shouldn't say, should he?

Why weren't the names public?

Had the police actually held up their part of the deal, and let the man and woman go, records a clean slate, even though they'd caused the death of over fifty police officers?

"Who was it?" Anouk repeated. "Why are you protecting them?"

"I'm not. I'm just…" Completely lost. Yosu had no idea what to do, or what to think.

"You said your trigger-happy youngster was part of the survivors," Anouk said. "How come he made it when so many others died?"

Yosu's voice was flat, reflecting his heart. "He made it to a survival dinghy in time. Managed to eject before the whole thing blew up."

"How did *you* survive?"

Yosu's shoulders slumped. "I carried a survival 'chute. It's part of the captain's uniform. When the explosion of the engines didn't kill me, I just floated around in the 'chute until the ambulance picked me up."

"And the cook?"

Yosu managed a little smile. "The cook has wonderful survival instincts. When we closed in on Barberousse, she was already in a survival dinghy, ready to press 'eject' if anything 'explosivy' happened. Her words."

"And the snitches? Whoever they are," Anouk added in a whisper.

"They wore police-issued survival 'chutes. Part of the deal they brokered, apparently."

"So you weren't the one to negotiate with them."

Yosu shook his head vehemently. "I just went after Barberousse at the coordinates they gave us."

Silence descended as Yosu relived—for the millionth time—the short-lived fight that cost so many lives.

Anouk's clear eyes bore into Yosu. "This is why you don't want any responsibilities anymore—don't bother denying it, the whole crew knows—because you feel responsible for what happened to your crew and my dad's?"

Closing his eyes, Yosu nodded.

"You *do* realize you were set up?"

Yosu's eyes snapped up to meet hers. "What?"

Anouk held up her hand to start ticking off points on her fingers. "The guy who started the whole thing survived. The snitches survived. The fact that they were snitches in the first place is not part of the public record." She lowered her hand. "How long did it take for backup to arrive once all hell broke loose?"

Yosu only managed a whisper. "Maybe thirty minutes."

"And what's the usual response time in that part of the universe?"

"At least twenty-four hours." Risks be damned, Yosu pulled out his chewing gum and bit into it. "Are you saying they were waiting nearby, knowing there'd be a fight?"

Anouk pursed her lips. "It sure seems like it. That way they get to clean up anything that might need it. They get to save the people doing their dirty work. And they get go play heroes for saving the valiant captain."

Yosu chewed at top speed. "Why would they even let me live?"

Shrugging, Anouk said, "Probably didn't see the harm in it. And removing the 'chute from your uniform would look suspicious. Besides, you haven't caused them much trouble since then, have you?"

Yosu let out a long, deep breath. "I sure haven't."

Anouk tapped the fingers of her right hand on the table, making a staccato beat that reminded Yosu of military marches.

"Maybe it's time you did," she said. "Find out who's responsible for killing your crew and causing you such pains."

Yosu stopped chewing. "I couldn't…"

"Tell me one thing." Anouk leaned forward across the table, her eyes deadly serious. "Do you still feel guilty? Responsible for all those people's deaths?"

Yosu was about to answer an automatic *yes*, but when he felt through that part of his chest, where he usually carried his guilt, it was much lighter. Some guilt remained—after, all, he should still have gotten the loose cannon off the team, and he should have asked the gunner to keep a closer eye on him. But that big, black ball of guilt and shame that had been eating him up from the inside? Gone.

"I don't," he replied, the surprise and awe clear in his voice.

"Then go back to taking charge. Let's find the corrupt bastards who killed my dad and your crew. Let's make them pay."

Yosu felt so lightened by his lifted burden, he was surprised he wasn't floating around, bumping into the ceiling. He didn't have to punish himself for what happened? External forces had *wanted* for that catastrophe to happen?

If knowing that made him feel this good, imagine what catching the culprits would do.

"I'm in."

AUTHOR'S NOTE

THANK YOU FOR reading *Common Enemies*. I hope you enjoyed the story.

If you liked the story, you might want to check out the other stories of the Lollapalooza short story series. The adventure continues as Yosu, Anouk, and the captain try to figure out what happened the day Yosu lost his team and Anouk her father.

I also write in a bunch of other genres. You can, for example, pick up the first book in my Tolosa Mystery series for free on my website.

R.W. Wallace
www.rwwallace.com

Also by R.W. Wallace

Mystery

The Tolosa Mystery Series
The Red Brick Haze (free)
The Red Brick Cellars
The Red Brick Basilica

Ghost Detective Shorts (coming soon)
Just Desserts
Lost Friends
Family Bonds
Till Death
Family History
Common Ground
Heritage
Eternal Bond
New Beginnings

Short Stories
Cold Blue Eternity
Hidden Horrors
Critters
Gertrude and the Trojan Horse
First Impressions
Let Them Eat Cake
Out of Sight
Two's Company
Like Mother Like Daughter

Fantasy (short stories)
Unexpected Consequences
Morbier Impossible
A Second Chance

Science Fiction (short stories)
The Vanguard

Lollapalooza Shorts
Quarantine
Common Enemies
Coiled Danger
Mars Meeting

Adventure (short stories)
Size Matters

ABOUT THE AUTHOR

R.W. WALLACE WRITES in most genres, though she tends to end up in mystery more often than not. Dead bodies keep popping up all over the place whenever she sits down in front of her keyboard.

The stories mostly take place in Norway or France; the country she was born in and the one that has been her home for two decades. Don't ask her why she writes in English – she won't have a sensible answer for you.

Her Ghost Detective short story series appears in *Pulphouse Magazine*, starting in issue #9.

www.rwwallace.com

www.ingramcontent.com/pod-product-compliance
Lightning Source LLC
LaVergne TN
LVHW041717060526
838201LV00043B/777